Doll Hospital™

Tatiana Comes to America

AN ELLIS ISLAND STORY

OTHER BOOKS IN THE
DOLL HOSPITAL SERIES

Doll Hospital #2
Goldie's Fortune

Doll Hospital #3
Glory's Freedom

♥ ♥ COMING SOON ♥ ♥

Doll Hospital #4
Saving Marissa

Doll Hospital #5

Doll Hospital #6

Doll Hospital™

Tatiana Comes to America

AN ELLIS ISLAND STORY

♥ ♥ ♥ ♥ ♥

BY JOAN HOLUB

Illustrations by Ann Iosa

A LITTLE APPLE PAPERBACK

SCHOLASTIC INC.

New York Toronto London Auckland Sydney
Mexico City New Delhi Hong Kong Buenos Aires

ISBN 0-439-40178-X

Design by Steve Scott

12 11 10 9 8 7 6 5 4 3 2 1 3 4 5 6 7/0

40

Printed in the U.S.A.
First Scholastic printing, July 2002

For Joy Peskin, who thought of doll hospitals.

With thanks to my mom for taking me and my doll Annie to a doll hospital.
—J.H.

Table of Contents

Doll Hospital™

Tatiana Comes to America

AN ELLIS ISLAND STORY

CHAPTER 1
To Grandmother's House We Go

♥ ♥ ♥ ♥ ♥

"A girl at school said her grandmother's house stinks like wet dog," said Rose from the backseat of the car.

Lila pulled her nose in from the side window and stopped munching her animal crackers. She clutched the little electronic toy dog hanging on her necklace. "I like dogs."

Rose frowned at her little sister, Lila.

"But not stink," Lila added quickly.

"Trust me. Your grandmother's house doesn't stink," said their mother. She didn't even look up from the map she was studying in the front seat.

"How do you know?" asked Rose.

"I grew up there, remember?" said their mom.

"Next exit, Robert!" she said to their dad. "Then through those woods. My, this area has changed. I hardly recognize any landmarks from the old neighborhood."

"Over the freeway and through the woods, to

Grandmother's house we go," sang Lila. She smiled at Rose, trying to cheer her up.

Rose sang back, "Mom has the map. It's in her lap . . ."

". . . And Dad drives very slow, ho!" added Lila.

Rose smiled for real for the first time that day. Every now and then, for a second, she could pretend that their parents weren't doctors going to Africa. That they weren't deserting Lila and her at their grandmother's. That they weren't ruining her summer, not to mention all of next year.

But then she would remember her mission. Lila was just a little kid. So Rose figured it was up to her to stop her mom and dad from leaving. And time was running out.

"I don't see why you have to be gone a whole year. Fifty-two looong weeks. Three hundred and sixty-five slooow days," Rose whined.

Their mom turned the rearview mirror and gave Rose The Eye.

Rose saw but pretended not to.

"Let's see. How many hours is that?" Rose looked at Lila.

"Too many," said Lila.

"Right," said Rose.

"We're going to miss you girls, too. But we'll be back before you know it," said their mom. "And staying with your grandmother for a year will be fun. Like going to camp."

"Camp Stink," said Rose.

Lila giggled. "Camp Stink-o-grama-rama."

"Girls!" scolded their mom.

"Okay. I'm just saying, if it stinks, I'm outta there," said Rose.

"Me, too," said Lila. "It's okay if Far Nana has a dog, though. Just not the stinky kind."

They called their dad's mother Near Nana because she lived near their apartment back in the city. But Near Nana lived in a building that was just for older people. It didn't allow kids. So while their parents were working in Africa, Rose and Lila were getting stuck with Far Nana. And they didn't even know her!

"Why haven't we ever met Far Nana before?" Rose grumped. "Is something wrong with her?"

"Don't be silly. You met her five years ago when she came to visit. Rose, you were five then. And Lila, you must have been three," said their mom. "She and I keep in touch by phone. It's true you haven't seen much of her. But that's only because she lives five hundred miles away from us."

Rose racked her brain for more ideas to stop her parents' plan. Too bad pretending to be sick was out. That never worked when you had doctors for parents.

"Why can't the Africa people get their own doctors?" asked Lila.

Rose smiled at Lila. "Good question."

"Hmmm?" said their dad.

Rose and Lila looked at each other. Most of their dad might be sitting in the car, but his brain was already in Africa.

"She *said*, why can't the Africa people get their own doctors," said Rose. "Why do you have to go?"

"Or why can't we go with you? Don't people in Africa like kids?" asked Lila.

"You know why. We've talked about all this before. Your mom and I are going to Africa to train other doctors to treat disease. The village we'll be in is too dangerous for you kids. And it's so distant."

"A 3-D reason," counted Lila. "Disease. Danger. Distance."

"So that's why we're leaving you with your grandmother for a year. She's looking forward to your visit," said their mom.

"I do believe we're here," announced their dad.

And right smack in the middle of nowhere, he stopped the car.

CHAPTER 2
Banana

♥ ♥ ♥ ♥ ♥

"We're here!" said their mom. "Come on, girls. We're running late."

"Cool! What a spooky-looking house!" said Lila. She bounced out of the car and grabbed her scooter from the trunk. Their dad got the rest of Rose and Lila's stuff out.

Rose opened the car door and stared out gloomily. They were parked in front of a big gray-and-white house. "I hope she at least has a big-screen TV," Rose muttered.

Lila opened the gate and scootered up the walk. "Over the sidewalk and up the steps, to Grandmother's porch we go," she sang.

Rose trailed like a snail behind her. Even she had to admit the house was cool, though. It was two stories, with a big round turret.

Rose touched some pale gray curlicues on the house's porch. "What's all this swirly stuff?"

“That’s called gingerbread,” began their mother.

Lila touched it, too. “It feels like wood, not gingerbread.”

The front door squeaked open. There stood a thin woman with a long braid and a velvety hat. Her glasses were gator green, with sparkly tips. Her tie-dyed scarves swirled and her beaded necklaces rattled when she moved.

“Mom!” Their mother hugged the woman in the doorway.

Lila leaned around them and stuck her head into the house. She sniffed. Then she elbowed Rose. “No stink.”

“Huh?” Rose was too busy staring to check for stink. She couldn’t believe it. Her grandmother was a hippie!

“Here they are, Mom — Rose and Lila,” their mother said to Far Nana.

“They’ve grown up!” said Far Nana. Their dad arrived and dropped their bags on the wooden porch. Far Nana hugged him, too. She didn’t hug Rose or Lila. That was okay with Rose. She didn’t like hugging strangers. And that’s what her grandmother was.

“I’m so sorry we have to rush off like this,” her mom told Far Nana. “I wanted you and the girls to get to know each other a little better before we left. But we should get going so we have enough time to check in at the airport . . .” Her voice trailed off.

Their dad nudged their mom. "We'll be leaving *present*-ly, right?" he said.

"Oh, right!" said their mother, like she'd just remembered something. She went deep-purse diving with one hand. After digging around in her huge pocketbook, she came up with two small boxes. She handed one to Rose and one to Lila. "We meant to give these to you girls earlier, but we got such a late start this morning."

"Presents!" cooed Lila.

"Open them," said their mom.

Rose tore off the ribbon and paper. Inside the box was a golden, heart-shaped locket.

Lila peeked over. "Hey! We got the same thing!"

Rose popped her locket open with her thumbnail. Lila copied her. One side of each locket held a picture of their mom. The other side had a picture of their dad.

"And see, I'm wearing a locket like yours, too," said their mom. "Mine has pictures of you two. Rose on one side, and Lila on the other. Every night, Dad and I will look at your pictures before we go to bed."

"We'll give you each a kiss," said their dad.

"You can do the same with our pictures," said their mom.

"Cool!" said Lila. She looped her locket around her neck. It clinked against her electronic toy dog.

Rose didn't say anything. She dribbled the chain of

her new necklace into one hand and wrapped her fingers tight around the locket.

Their dad touched their mom's shoulder. "We've got to get going," he reminded her.

Their mom hugged Lila. "C'mon. Give us a hug big enough to last a year."

Lila hugged them back hard. First Mom, then Dad. "Banana," she said.

When they were little, Rose and Lila had learned that "*Hasta mañana*" meant "See you tomorrow" in Spanish. Lila had shortened it to "banana." Either way, Rose knew they wouldn't be seeing their parents tomorrow.

Mom and Dad hugged Rose, too, but she didn't hug back. Maybe they would get the message that she was mad. Maybe they would stay so they could all talk about it.

But that didn't happen.

"We'll call when we get there," promised their mom.

Rose sensed her parents slipping away. Trying to hold onto them was like trying to hold onto wet noodles. Suddenly things started moving fast. Their parents were moving down the sidewalk. Then their car was moving. Away.

Then their parents left. Just like they'd said they would when they'd told Rose and Lila about Africa a month ago.

Rose and Lila ran to the gate and watched the car fade down the street.

"Mom! Dad!" Rose whispered. "Come back!"

"I can't believe they're gone," said Lila.

Rose sniffled and then made herself stop. "Me, either."

Lila squished closer beside Rose at the gate. She held out her box of animal crackers. "Footsies?"

Rose took the box and looked inside. All that was left were animal feet. Rose liked the feet best. Lila knew that.

Even though she wasn't hungry, Rose munched the feet Lila had given her. The locket was digging into her hand, so she looped it around her neck. She popped it open and stared at the pictures of her mom and dad. They were upside down. She turned the locket to see them the right way.

Rose wished she had hugged them. Now it was too late.

CHAPTER 3

The Witch's Hat

♥ ♥ ♥ ♥ ♥

Rose and Lila stood at the gate for a long time. Then they headed back inside. Not because they wanted to. Because it was getting dark. And they had nowhere else to go.

Far Nana had been watching from the porch swing. The minute Rose and Lila started up the sidewalk, she hopped up, beads rattling. She held the front door open wide for them.

Lila looked around. "Where's our stuff?" It was gone from the porch, where their dad had left it.

"I put it in your mother's old room," Far Nana said. "I thought you'd enjoy staying there. Come on. I'll show you." She was smiling a fakey smile. Rose noticed she kept twisting and untwisting her beads. Maybe she was nervous, too.

Rose and Lila followed Far Nana up the stairs to the second floor. A smaller set of winding stairs continued up. Rose heard scuffling sounds up there. She peered into the gloom but couldn't see where the steps ended.

"What's up those stairs?" she asked.

"That's the witch's hat," said Far Nana.

Lila's eyes got big. She loved spooky stuff. "Witch's hat?"

"It's the turret with the tall, pointy roof," explained Far Nana. "Everyone in the neighborhood calls it that because it looks like a witch's hat from the outside. It's had the nickname for so long I'd forgotten how strange it must sound to newcomers."

They went down the hall and turned left. Far Nana opened a door and waved them in. "This is where your mother grew up."

Rose and Lila stepped inside and looked around.

On one side of the room was a cozy nook with a window seat. Outside the window's lacy curtains stood a big old tree. A round braided rug covered most of the wood floor. There were some bookshelves and an old trunk by the bunk beds.

"Bunk beds!" Lila ran for the ladder and hopped onto the top bunk. "Dibs!" she said.

"Our mom had bunk beds when she was little?" asked Rose.

Far Nana smiled, like she was remembering a long time ago. "Yes, she liked to trade off. Sometimes she slept up. Sometimes down."

Rose sat on the bottom bunk. It was hard to imagine their mom living in this room and sleeping in bunk beds.

"I kept a lot of your mother's stuff, so you girls might like to poke around in here. You can explore the rest of the house tomorrow," she told them.

"I want to see the witch's hat. I'll bet we can spy on the whole town from up there," said Lila.

"Oh, the witch's hat is off-limits to anyone but me," said Far Nana.

Off-limits? Rose and Lila gave each other a secret look. Ha! Not for long, they said in silent sister brainwave talk. They'd snoop later.

For now, Rose did have one big question that couldn't wait.

"Um, I was wondering something," she said to Far Nana. "What kind of TV do you have?"

Far Nana looked surprised. "Oh, I don't have one."

"No TV?" Rose and Lila said at the same time.

"What about a computer?" asked Rose.

"I don't have a computer, either," said Far Nana. She was twisting her beads again.

Lila leaned her head down from the top bunk. She looked at Rose like she expected her to make Far Nana get a TV. Her eyes were huge. So were Rose's.

Nobody said anything for a few long seconds. Far Nana kept twisting her beads as she backed out of the room.

"Well, I've got work to do in the witch's hat this evening, so I'll say good night," she said a little too cheerfully. "My room is at the other end of the hall. Let me know if you need anything."

"I need a big-screen TV is what I need," Rose grumbled after Far Nana had gone. "And a computer."

"Yeah," said Lila. "Maybe she was kidding. Not everybody has a computer. But everybody has a TV, don't they?"

Rose flopped on her bed like a drama queen. "I knew this house was weird."

"Did you hear what Mom called it?" Lila whispered after a minute. "A gingerbread house. Like in *Hansel and Gretel.* And guess who lived in the gingerbread house."

Rose didn't have to guess. She knew.

A witch. A hippie witch.

CHAPTER 4

A Hospital for Dolls

♥ ♥ ♥ ♥ ♥

Rose counted thirteen stairs.

Creeeaak! She pushed open the door to the witch's hat an inch at a time. Finally it was open enough for her to slip inside.

She stood still while her eyes got used to the dark. Turning on the light might wake Far Nana.

Creeeaak! Bony fingers brushed her arm. The light snapped on.

Aghhh! Rose screamed.

Aghhh! someone screamed back. It was Lila!

Lila bumped into a shelf, and they both fell to the floor in a heap.

Little round blue-and-white balls bounced everywhere around them. Rose picked one up and quickly threw it away. "Gross!"

It was raining eyeballs!

Rose and Lila jumped up and stared in amazement. All around them were dolls. And parts of dolls. Arms. Legs. Heads. And — eyeballs!

Lila gasped. "Our grandmother is a doll murderer!"

"Why did you sneak up on me like that?" said Rose. "You ruined everything."

"You sneaked first. I just followed you up the stairs to see where you were sneaking to."

"Shhh! She'll hear us," said Rose.

"Too late. She's already heard you," said Far Nana as she stepped inside the door.

"Uh-oh. Now we're in for it," said Lila. She scooted behind Rose.

Far Nana went down the hall and got a broom. Then she started sweeping up eyeballs. Rose and Lila crawled around on the floor, helping.

"What are you doing up here? You almost gave me a heart attack. I thought you were burglars," said Far Nana.

She sounded sleepy, not mad. But just in case, Rose decided to try to take her mind off their sneaking.

"Are all these dolls yours?" she asked.

Far Nana stopped sweeping. "Some of them."

"I thought dolls were for kids," said Lila.

"This is my doll hospital," explained Far Nana. "People bring me their broken dolls, and I fix them."

"I've never heard of a hospital for dolls," said Lila.

"Your mother and father are doctors who fix people," said Far Nana. "I'm a doll doctor. I fix dolls. It's my gift."

"Why did you try to keep it a secret?" Rose asked.

Far Nana looked surprised. "I didn't. I'm proud of my work."

"Then why did you tell us the witch's hat was off-limits?" asked Rose.

"I guess I'm used to living alone," Far Nana said. "I don't let many people come up here. I don't want anyone messing up the place."

The shelves in the room were full of boxes and bags of doll stuff. There were buttons, eyeballs, shoes, and wigs everywhere. It already looked pretty messy in there. Rose and Lila didn't say so, though. They didn't want to hurt Far Nana's feelings.

There were lots of dolls, too. Big dolls, little dolls, in-between-sized dolls.

One of them caught Rose's eye. It had wavy blond hair and blue eyes. And a big crack in its face. The crack reminded Rose of Humpty-Dumpty.

"What happened to this one?" she asked.

"Ah! That's Tatiana." Far Nana lifted the doll from the shelf. She turned it toward Rose and Lila so they could see it better. "She's pretty, isn't she?"

Rose and Lila gave each other quick sideways looks. The doll was in bad shape. Couldn't Far Nana see that?

Rose tried to be polite. "Sort of. I guess she used to be beautiful. But now her face is cracked."

Lila wrinkled her nose. "And her clothes are kind of raggedy."

Far Nana waved her hand as though to say those things didn't matter. "I'll fix all that soon enough. You have to look beyond her cracked face to see her true beauty. Tatiana is beautiful inside, too. She has just had a hard life."

"How do you know?" asked Lila.

Far Nana fluffed out Tatiana's skirt. "She told me."

"What?" asked Rose.

Far Nana put a hand over her mouth like she wished she could take back her words. "Uh, I mean . . ."

Lila searched all over the doll, looking for a switch or a pull cord. "What do you mean? Does she talk, like my electronic dog?"

"Well, in a way," said Far Nana. She looked like she was trying to think up a lie.

"In what way?" insisted Rose. She wanted to know what Far Nana was hiding. "Come on. Tell us what happened to her. *Puhleeeze*?"

"Yeah," added Lila. "Why is she all cracked up?"

Far Nana ran her fingers through her hair. It was still braided, but lots of it had come loose. "Uh — I haven't asked her yet. I mean . . ."

"You mean you talk to dolls?" Rose asked.

Far Nana sat in a wooden rocking chair and sighed. "Yes."

"No way," said Rose.

"Show us," said Lila.

Far Nana pulled a cord on a lamp beside the chair. Green goo inside the lamp began slithering around. "All right," she said. "I guess there's no harm in showing you. First, turn off the overhead light. This LAVA lamp will be enough."

Lila jumped up and turned off the wall switch. Then it was dark except for the ghostly green glow from the LAVA lamp.

"Okay, go," said Rose. She couldn't wait to see what Far Nana was going to do.

Far Nana set the doll in her lap so it faced her. Her fingers cupped Tatiana's head gently. She stared into the doll's eyes.

"Tell us your story," she whispered.

It gave Rose the willies. Far Nana didn't really expect the doll to talk by herself, did she? Rose peeked over at Lila. Lila looked thrilled at the spooky turn of events. It figured.

Nothing happened for a few seconds.

Then Far Nana began to speak.

CHAPTER 5

My Girl

Tatiana's Story

♥ ♥ ♥ ♥ ♥

My girl's name was Anya. She called me her doll. I called her my girl. When I came to live with her, she gave me my name, Tatiana.

Anya's clown puppet did not believe this, but sometimes I thought Anya could almost hear me when I spoke to her. She was a special girl, and I was lucky to have her for my own. However, I hadn't always lived with Anya.

My first home was a toy shop in a large Russian town. It was an easy life. For many days, I sat on a pillow with silk tassels in the shop window. On one side of me stood a charming nutcracker, with a dark mustache and a red uniform. And on the other side was a set of five colorful nesting dolls. They were chatterboxes and lively company.

We passed the days watching the comings and goings outside our window.

Milk and bread deliveries came early each morning by horse-drawn wagon.

Across the street, beyond the big fountain, was a hat shop. Hats with ribbons, feathers, and flowers hung in its windows. We often played a game, trying to guess which hat a woman would buy when she entered the store.

In the evenings, fancy carriages went to and fro on the cobblestone streets. Ladies dressed in satin and gentlemen with silk ties rode inside the carriages. I liked to imagine the exciting parties they might be going to.

I was happy for a time, living among my own kind.

But day by day it grew colder in our toy shop window.

People out in the streets bundled up, wearing long scarves and woolen coats. I dreaded the arrival of customers. Each one brought a fresh swirl of frosty air inside the shop. No one offered me a coat, so I just shivered in my thin, lacy blouse.

One cold and dreary day, a gray-haired woman came into the shop. I had seen her before, with a little girl. The girl had often looked at me with longing as I sat in the window. That did not make her unusual. Many stopped to stare at me, for I am quite beautiful.

Some thought my face was china. However, it is actually bisque. My cheeks were a soft pink blush. Blue beads were woven through my wavy blond hair. Sparkly glass earrings hung from my pierced ears. My ruffled blue velvet skirt was edged with shiny satin ribbon. Soft leather boots with buttons peeked from below my skirt. I was the height of fashion in 1907.

On this day, the bell tinkled as the gray-haired woman came inside, alone. To my surprise, the shop owner lifted me from my home in the window. He handed me to the woman, who examined me carefully. She even pulled up my skirt to count my petticoats!

The woman nodded as though pleased. Then she gave the shop owner some coins. I quickly found myself wrapped in paper and tied with string.

The bell tinkled, and I could tell the woman had carried me outside. But I couldn't see a thing from inside my paper prison. It was terrifying!

Strange noises and smells came at me from every direction. Horses clip-clopped down the cobblestone streets. Bits of conversations and the calls of vendors selling their wares floated past. I smelled evergreen trees and roasting chestnuts.

Eventually, I heard a door open. I felt a warm rush of air. Then there was silence. Exhausted, I slept.

CHAPTER 6

Friends Forever

Tatiana's Story

♥ ♥ ♥ ♥ ♥

I remained wrapped in paper for days. The time passed slowly.

At some point I heard noise again. It was the sound of laughter and music. Happy sounds. Children sounds.

Soon the paper and string around me were ripped away. I was free!

The sudden light blinded me at first. My eyes had become used to the darkness inside my wrappings.

"Oh, thank you, Father!" I heard a girl say.

Within seconds, my eyes got used to the light. A little girl was holding me. It was the same girl who had often admired me in the shop window. Other children crowded around to see me. I felt a little shy at the sight of so many strange new faces.

A man leaned over the girl's shoulder to see me, too. He had a dark beard and mustache. He reminded me a bit of my old friend the nutcracker.

"Let me see the gift I bought you, Anya," he said.

So the girl's name is Anya, I thought. I looked around for clues that would explain my new situation. I saw a cake and a pile of paper and ribbons. Aha! I was at a birthday party! Now I understood. I was Anya's birthday present from her father.

I relaxed for the first time in days. I had been so worried about what would become of me. Young Anya had gentle hands and a kind voice. I was no longer afraid.

"Baba said you often stopped to see a pretty doll in the toy shop," Anya's father said. "So of course I told her to buy this doll for my only daughter. And you have good taste. Your new doll is a pretty one."

The gray-haired woman who had bought me at the toy shop came to stand beside Anya and her father. When she smiled, her eyes almost disappeared into the wrinkles on her face. Now I realized this must be Anya's grandmother, her baba.

"What will you call her?" Anya's grandmother asked.

Anya's soft brown eyes looked deep into my blue ones. "I will call you Tatiana," she whispered. "We will be friends forever."

CHAPTER 7

Anya's Favorite

Tatiana's Story

♥ ♥ ♥ ♥ ♥

I quickly became used to my new life with Anya.

At times I missed my old friends at the toy shop. Did they worry about me? There was no way to let them know I was happy and well. So I simply tried not to think about them.

Instead I set about making friends with Anya's other toys. Her clown puppet only smiled when Anya came around and was not pleasant otherwise. But the others made me feel welcome.

Anya's nesting dolls were not as talkative as those in the toy shop. Still, they were a nice family. Most nesting dolls are kind and good-natured, I've found. They showed me around Anya's room and answered any questions I had. From them I learned that Anya's mother had died years ago, that Anya's last name was Peskin, and other useful information.

Luckily, no one seemed jealous that I was Anya's favorite. And I was.

My girl showered me with gifts. I soon had a leather trunk full of clothes. Anya gave me six dresses, some of which she made herself with Baba's help. My favorite gown was made of green velvet, covered with seed pearls. I had a hand-painted fan, long gloves, and a parasol to match. I even had my own hand mirror, with real mirrored glass!

Anya took me everywhere she went. We often visited her friend Sasha Levov, who lived nearby. I enjoyed showing off my pretty outfits and trading gossip with Sasha's dolls on our visits.

Several times a week, we went to the frozen pond in the park. Anya wrapped me in a shawl and set me on the bench beside Baba. She knew I would enjoy watching the ice-skaters. My Anya was kind in many ways. More than once, I saw her help the youngest skaters. She lifted one boy who had fallen on the ice. She took his hand, and they skated side by side. He was soon laughing.

It was a happy time.

But it was not to last forever.

The days turned warmer. Even so, Anya's father told us not to go out on our own.

"Pogroms," he explained. "The Russian czar's Cossack soldiers are attacking villages. They don't like us Jews. We don't know what's coming next. You must stay close to home, where I know you are safe."

In early summer, Baba caught a terrible cold. Anya read to her each morning as Baba lay in bed under warm quilts. She even brought her soup in the afternoons.

Our days passed quietly.

CHAPTER 8
Trouble
Tatiana's Story

♥ ♥ ♥ ♥ ♥

Late one night there was a knock at the door. Anya was asleep. I had been thinking about the events of the past afternoon.

Anya's friend Sasha had come over with her favorite doll, Lise. We had enjoyed a lovely tea party in the warm sunshine of the garden. Lise and I had even made a new friend, a funny black squirrel.

I heard the rumble of voices downstairs after Anya's father answered the door.

I recognized the visitor's voice. It was Sasha's father, Mr. Levov. I lay very still, trying to overhear what was going on.

"There's trouble," Mr. Levov told Anya's father. "Cossack soldiers have raided a village only twenty miles away. Our town may be next."

Suddenly I realized Anya was awake. She lifted me from my pillow, and we sneaked down the stairs to listen.

". . . Russia is not safe for Jews as long as Czar Nicholas II rules," Mr. Levov was saying.

Anya's father's bushy eyebrows frowned. I had never seen him afraid. His fear made me afraid, too.

"I am taking my family to safety," Mr. Levov went on. "We are going to America. We are going to get away from the Cossacks while we still can."

"How soon?" asked Anya's father.

"We leave tonight," said Mr. Levov.

"Tonight?" echoed Anya's father.

Mr. Levov nodded. "There is no time to waste. Come with us."

Anya's father shook his head. "I can't. Baba is better, but she is still too ill to travel."

"You are risking your life by staying," said Mr. Levov. "I will pray for you." He turned to go.

Her father laid a hand on Mr. Levov's shoulder to stop him. "Wait! Take Anya. Take my daughter to America."

"No!" Anya shouted. "I want to stay with you and Baba!"

Anya's father and Mr. Levov turned toward us in surprise. Anya flew down the stairs and into her father's arms. He hugged her but ignored her words.

"My brother Elias already lives in New York," he told Mr. Levov. "He and his family will care for Anya until Baba and I can come to America, too."

"No, Father!" shouted Anya.

Baba pulled Anya away from her father and patted her back gently. She had heard the noise and had come out of her room to see what was going on. "Listen to your father," said Baba. "He is trying to do what is best for all of us."

Anya sobbed.

Mr. Levov nodded. "All right. I will take Anya. With my eight children, one more will not make a difference."

Baba helped Anya dress and pack. When we came back downstairs with our bag, Anya's father tried to grab me away from her.

"Take only what you can carry. There's no room for toys," he told her.

"No! Please! Let me take Tatiana," begged Anya. "I can carry her."

Her father sighed and rubbed one hand over his face. He smiled sadly at Anya. Then he opened his arms. She ran into them.

"All right," he whispered. "Take Tatiana. Maybe she will keep you safe."

I will try, I promised. I wished with all my might to make him hear.

Anya's father tucked an envelope into her bag.

"The Levovs will deliver you to your Uncle Elias. This letter will explain everything to him. He will take you to live with his family. It is only until Baba and I can come to America, too. Do not lose this letter, Anya."

Anya nodded. "Come with us, Father. Please!" she begged.

He shook his head no. "Be brave. Baba and I will come to America when we can."

We hugged Baba good-bye. Then Anya's father held us tight one last time. "I love you," he whispered.

And then he let us go.

We were off on our journey into the dark night. It would not be an easy one.

CHAPTER 9
Doll Fortune-teller

♥ ♥ ♥ ♥ ♥

Far Nana yawned two times in a row. Lila craned her neck, trying to count tooth fillings. That was one of Lila's weird hobbies.

"Enough for tonight. Let's all hit the sack," said Far Nana.

"What sack?" asked Lila.

"Bed," said Far Nana.

"But what happened to Anya and Tatiana?" asked Rose.

"Tomorrow," promised Far Nana. "It's nearly midnight. Tatiana is tired. And so am I."

"You can't stop now!" said Lila.

Rose frowned at Lila. They probably shouldn't make Far Nana mad. What if she threw them out into the cold, cruel world? They'd have to find relatives to go live with. Just like poor Anya.

"Come on." Rose hopped up and pulled Lila out the door. Together they went down the winding stairs. Far Nana followed close behind, yawning.

At the bottom of the stairs, Far Nana turned right. Rose and Lila turned left.

"Good night," called Far Nana. "Again."

"'Night," mumbled Rose and Lila.

They stumbled into their room and into bed, Rose in the bottom bunk and Lila in the top.

Click! Rose heard Lila open her locket. Lila's voice floated down from the top bunk. "Did you kiss Mom and Dad good night?"

"Yeah. You?" asked Rose.

"Yeah," said Lila. "I miss them."

Rose swallowed hard. She felt the sharp burn of tears in her eyes. "Me, too." She would *not* cry!

"Do you think Far Nana is making up Tatiana's story?" asked Lila.

"It sounded kind of real," said Rose. "But I don't know."

"If it is true, I wonder how she does it," said Lila. "Is she magic or something? Hey! Maybe she has ESP like Detecto-Dog on TV."

"Or maybe she has a crystal-doll-ball that helps her tell doll fortunes," said Rose.

"Madame Far Nana, Doll Fortune-teller," joked Lila.

Rose and Lila giggled. But they were both wondering the same thing: Could Far Nana really hear Tatiana? And if so, how did she do it?

Lila was quiet for a few minutes. Then she began speaking in a spooky voice. "What if one dark, stormy night Far Nana is in the witch's hat, and she needs some doll eyes. Only she can't find any. She might come looking for yours."

"Or yours," said Rose.

"Nope," said Lila. "My eyes are green. Didn't you notice? Those bouncing eyeballs were all blue ones. Like yours."

Rose shivered.

Honestly, Lila was the spookiest eight-year-old ever.

CHAPTER 10
Fend for Yourself

♥ ♥ ♥ ♥ ♥

The next morning Rose woke with a start. Something warm and heavy was lying on each of her feet. She shook them. The things didn't move. She wiggled her toes. Sharp needles dug in and pricked her.

Ahhhh! she shrieked.

Two furry beasts exploded from her bed. One was gray and one was black. They zoomed out the door.

"What?" Lila almost fell out of the upper bunk, trying to see what was happening.

Rose pointed toward the door.

Lila scrambled down the ladder and looked out into the hall.

"Cats!" she shouted. She did a happy dance. "Yahoo! Far Nana has cats!"

"You girls really are going to give me a heart attack," said Far Nana. She leaned against one side of their doorway.

Rose blinked at the sight of Far Nana's robe. It was

DAY-GLO purple, with big green flowers all over it. It was kind of hard to look at first thing in the morning.

"I didn't know you had cats. I *looove* cats!" said Lila. "Do you have dogs, too?"

Far Nana smiled. "No. Just four cats. John, Paul, George, and Ringo. Three are gray. Ringo's the black one."

Just then, Rose's stomach growled. She hoped no one heard.

"You girls hungry? What should we have for breakfast?" Far Nana headed down the hall. Rose and Lila followed her to the kitchen.

"What day is it?" asked Rose.

Far Nana thought for a minute. "Saturday."

"Saturday is FFY. Fend For Yourself," said Rose. "At least at our house it is. Was."

Far Nana looked confused.

"You know. We each get to choose whatever we want for breakfast. As long as we can make it by ourselves," said Lila.

"Oh. Okay," said Far Nana. "Go for it."

"I want crispy cardboard with slime," said Rose. She opened the cupboard and found the bread and jelly. "That's jelly toast."

"Drowning shredded feet for me," said Lila.

"That's cereal with milk," Rose explained. "You know, like shredded wheat. Want some?"

Far Nana looked a little dazed. "I think I'll stick with oatmeal."

Rose and Lila giggled.

Far Nana raised one eyebrow. "I supposed you have a nickname for that, too?"

They nodded. "Barf."

Far Nana made a yucky face, then burst out laughing. "Barf for breakfast. Yum! I learn something new every day."

After breakfast, they all got dressed and went up to the witch's hat.

CHAPTER 11

Falling Apart

♥ ♥ ♥ ♥ ♥

"When can we hear more of Tatiana's story?" asked Lila.

"Soon. First there's work to be done," said Far Nana. She took off Tatiana's skirt.

"Where are her petticoats? You said Baba counted them at the toy shop," said Rose.

Far Nana shrugged. "I guess they got lost over the years. We'll make some more, good as new." She removed the last of Tatiana's clothes.

"I thought all of Tatiana was made of china. But just part of her is," said Lila.

"She's bisque, not china. Remember?" said Rose.

"Bisque and china are pretty, but they break easily," explained Far Nana. "So bisque often was used only for a doll's head and shoulders. The rest of Tatiana is made of cloth and leather."

"The rest of her is falling apart!" said Lila.

It was true. Tatiana's body, upper arms, and legs were made of cloth. Sawdust oozed out of places where the cloth was thin or torn. Two safety pins held one big rip closed.

Tatiana's hands and shoes were made of dirty, faded leather. They were sewn to her cloth body. Some of the threads had come undone, so her hands and shoes flopped loosely.

"She's a mess," said Rose.

"I've seen worse," Far Nana said. "And we all get old sometime. Tatiana has lived a long, good life. More than twice as many years as me."

"Wow! How old *are* you?" asked Rose.

Far Nana ducked the question. "No time for chitchat. Now we clip here and here."

Snip! Far Nana cut threads in four places. The threads connected Tatiana's head and shoulders to her body. When they came loose, so did Tatiana's head.

"Off with her head!" said Lila.

Rose rolled her eyes. "This is kind of gross."

Far Nana laughed. She set Tatiana's body aside. "I'll repair the bisque first. By the time it's dry, the rest of her will be ready."

Rose and Lila watched as Far Nana mixed some light pinkish glop on a palette.

She carefully painted it on Tatiana's face and shoulders. She smoothed it out over and over with her wet fingers.

Then she set Tatiana's head inside a cabinet with glass doors. "So the cats won't get her," she explained.

Tatiana stared out at them through the glass.

CHAPTER 12

Spying

♥ ♥ ♥ ♥ ♥

Next, Far Nana showed Rose and Lila how to clean Tatiana's hands and shoes. She dipped a small sponge in a jar of cleaner and rubbed the leather parts. She let Rose and Lila practice on a scrap of old leather.

"Don't soak the sponge," Far Nana said. "You don't want to get the leather too wet."

Once Tatiana's hands and shoes were clean, Far Nana coated them with leather polish. Then she tied them to a coat hanger with thread and hung them up to dry.

"Tatiana's body is beyond repair," announced Far Nana. "So I'll have to make new cloth parts to wrap around her old ones."

"That sounds kind of hard. Why don't you just sew a new body?" asked Rose.

"A good doll doctor tries to save as much of an old doll as possible," explained Far Nana.

Far Nana got some old-looking fabric out of a drawer. She smoothed it out on her worktable.

"This is muslin," she told them. "I soaked it in weak tea to dye it the same color as Tatiana. Now I'm going to measure Tatiana's old body, arms, and legs. Then I'll make paper patterns and use those to cut new parts out of this cloth. I'll sew the new pieces over the old parts by hand. That way, most of the old Tatiana will be saved."

They worked in silence for a while. Rose and Lila handed tools to Far Nana as she needed them. Then they helped by scooping up stuffing that had fallen out of Tatiana's old body.

When Rose and Lila were done, Far Nana looked up. "Remaking the body may take a while. Do you girls want to run off and explore for a bit?"

"You won't listen to more of Tatiana's story without us, will you?" asked Rose.

"No, I'll call you first," promised Far Nana.

"Okay," said Rose.

Rose and Lila ran out. Then they ducked back in.

"Are you sure you don't have a TV?" asked Rose.

"Or a computer?" added Lila.

Far Nana shooed them out. "Go! Outside! Get some fresh air."

Rose and Lila went downstairs to snoop around a little. Long strings of beads hung down, filling the doorway to the living room. The beads swayed and clacked as Rose and Lila went through.

Inside, they found a record player and a bunch of old

records. Dozens of pin-on metal buttons were stuck to a bulletin board hanging on one wall. There were buttons with smiley faces, peace signs, and music groups Rose and Lila had never heard of.

Lila spun around and around in an orange swivel chair that looked like a big bowl.

Rose tried out a beanbag chair. "Far Nana has a lot of cool old stuff."

"Yeah," said Lila. She hopped up. "Let's go check out her yard. I want to see the witch's hat from the outside."

Rose wiggled up from the beanbag chair. It was harder to get out of than it had been to get into.

From across the street, the witch's hat looked even spookier. The whole house did. But staring at the house got boring after a while.

"It's noon-thirty. I'm missing *Real Pet Heroes* on TV," complained Lila.

Rose kicked a loose stone in the wall along one side of the house. "What are we supposed to do out here? This is CRUP."

Lila tried to figure out what the letters CRUP stood for. She couldn't. "I give up."

"CRuel and Unusual Punishment," said Rose.

"Good one," said Lila.

They both heard the bushes swish at the same time.

"Shhh!" Rose got down behind the railing and

waved at Lila to do the same. "Over by the bushes. There's a kid next door."

Lila squatted down. "Boy or girl?"

"Can't tell. Girl, I think," said Rose. "Yeah. She has long braids."

"What's she doing?"

"Don't know."

"What does it look like she's doing?" asked Lila.

Rose looked over the railing. "Spying on us. She has binoculars."

"Let's spy back on her then," said Lila.

Rose and Lila sneaked over to the hedge and peeked through.

"I hear you," said the next-door girl.

Rose and Lila kept quiet.

"You're not scaring me," said the girl.

"Oooooo," moaned Rose.

"Oooooo," echoed Lila.

"You're weird," said the girl.

Rose and Lila heard footsteps cross the grass. They stood up just as the door to the yellow house next door slammed shut.

CHAPTER 13

Slime and Rocks

♥ ♥ ♥ ♥ ♥

Rose and Lila got back to the witch's hat just in time to watch Far Nana put Tatiana back together.

Far Nana pointed toward a tray. "I made sandwiches for lunch," she told them. "They're on the TV tray. Take your pick."

"Why do you have a TV tray but no TV?" asked Lila.

Far Nana laughed. "Good question."

Rose picked up a jelly and crunchy peanut butter sandwich. "Umm! Slime and rocks."

"Moon cheese for me," said Lila, choosing a sandwich of holey Swiss cheese.

While Rose and Lila munched, Far Nana sewed. Hands went onto arms and shoes went onto legs. She took Tatiana's head out of the glass case and stitched it back on to her body.

Finally, Tatiana was back to normal.

"There, I think Tatiana is feeling more like herself now," said Far Nana.

"Is she ready to talk again?" Rose asked Far Nana.

"I think so. I'll mend her clothes while we chat with her," said Far Nana.

Lila lay on her back on the floor and got comfortable. She lifted one of the gray cats onto her chest. "Hi, George," she said. Rose wondered how Lila knew which cat was which. The only one she knew for sure was Ringo, the black one.

"Can I sew something?" Rose asked Far Nana.

"Not this time," said Far Nana. "But we'll practice sewing, and maybe you can help some other time."

"Okay." Rose hoped she meant it. She snuggled into a fan-backed wicker chair. Ringo leaped into her lap. Another cat curled around the back of her chair. Rose wasn't sure which one.

Cat number four had found a leftover doll eyeball on the floor and was playing soccer with it. Lila laughed. She was in cat heaven. She wiggled her feet onto the chair seat beside Rose. Rose scooted over a little so Lila's feet had enough room.

They waited for Far Nana to begin.

Far Nana pulled a pretty wool shawl from a coatrack behind the door. She wrapped Tatiana in it. "That'll keep her warm while she's waiting for her new clothes."

She placed Tatiana on a pillow by the window. A soft pool of light lit Tatiana's face. She seemed to glow.

Far Nana stared deep into the doll's blue eyes. "Tell me your story," she whispered.

A minute later, Far Nana once again began to speak.

CHAPTER 14
A Long Journey
Tatiana's Story

♥ ♥ ♥ ♥ ♥

The night sky was black and starless.

Mr. Levov lifted us into his wagon. Mrs. Levov pulled her children around her in the wagon bed. We huddled in beside them, close to Sasha.

"Keep your heads down," Mr. Levov told us. Then he and Sasha's oldest brother, Jacob, flicked the reins. The horses began pulling our wagon.

I tried not to think of my beautiful hand mirror, parasol, and dresses. Or Anya's other toys. They had all been left behind. Just like our old lives.

Anya held me close, but I peeked out over her arm. In the distance, I saw smoke. What was burning?

I would soon see.

Our wagon bounced along through town and past the big fountain. The streets began to look familiar. We were nearing my former home, the toy shop.

Soon I would see the nutcracker and nesting dolls

again! I turned to wave at my old friends in the shop window.

And I gasped in horror.

Fiery flames danced in the very window where I had once sat. The shop's glass window had been smashed.

My friends! What had happened to them?

We passed the toy shop too quickly. I had no chance to look closer. Still, I feared my old friends were no more. They could not have survived such a disaster.

Months had gone by since I had seen them last. Perhaps in that time they had found good homes, as I had with Anya. Perhaps they were safe. I hoped it was so.

We traveled all night. By early morning, we reached the train station.

I did not want to go anywhere near the train. It looked to me to be a giant black monster. However, I was given no say, and we all got on.

Black smoke whooshed from the engine, and a bell clanged. The train swayed and began to move along the tracks. It traveled faster than any carriage! I found its speed alarming and thrilling at the same time.

All of us sat close together on the train's bench seats. We were quiet, except for the youngest children. They played in the aisle. Anya and I were tired and we slept.

Our days on the train blurred from one into the next. On the fourth day, I noticed an odd, fishy smell. I knew that smell. It reminded me of the fish vendor. He had often visited the toy shop to chat with the shopkeeper.

Anya and I looked out the window. A huge steamship with three gleaming red smokestacks was docked in the harbor. We had reached the ocean!

CHAPTER 15

On Our Way

Tatiana's Story

♥ ♥ ♥ ♥ ♥

Anya had to help Sasha and her mother with the younger Levov children so she tucked me inside her bag for a while. I understood. There are times when I can be a burden.

While I was packed away, we boarded the steamship. Anya took me out again once we were inside our cabin. It was on the upper deck of the ship and looked quite comfortable. A window with flowered curtains let in lots of sunshine. There was a wooden chest of drawers, a washstand with an oval mirror, and three beds. We were sharing with Sasha and her older sister, Kira.

We stayed in our cabin just long enough to get settled. Then Anya burst out the door and ran across the wooden deck of the ship.

Outside, the wind was fresh and clean. We had been trapped on the train for so long! It felt wonderful to be free.

Sasha, her brother Jacob, and Mr. Levov stood at the

railing. We joined them. More people were boarding the ship on the deck below. It was fun to watch.

The people below formed a long line up the ship's gangplank. There were hundreds of them. Women in scarves. Men in dark hats. And most of all, children.

Sasha pointed at one of them. "Look at that girl in the yellow scarf. Her face and legs are skinny. But she is fat around the middle!"

"She's not fat. She is wearing many dresses at once!" said Jacob. Jacob and Sasha laughed.

The girl in the yellow scarf heard. She turned and waved.

Anya waved back.

The girl went through a door and disappeared. One by one, the rest of the people in line disappeared through the door, too.

"Where are they all going?" wondered Sasha.

"Into the bottom of the ship. They are traveling in third class. It's called steerage," said Jacob.

"How do they all fit down there?" asked Anya.

"It's crowded," said Mr. Levov. "Steerage is not fit for humans."

"Why don't they come up here?" suggested Anya. "There's plenty of room."

Mr. Levov and Jacob laughed.

"Not everyone can afford to pay forty American dollars to sail in first class as we do," said Mr. Levov. "It

only costs ten dollars to travel in steerage. They try to stand it for the two weeks it takes to get to America."

Hooo! Hooo! A loud whistle blew. Anya and Sasha covered their ears.

Our steamship began chugging out of the harbor. Thick smoke puffed from its red smokestacks.

Anya grew quiet. I knew she was missing her father. "I wonder what America looks like," she said.

"When you see Lady Liberty, you will know you are in America. She stands at America's entrance to welcome us," said Mr. Levov.

"In America, there are buildings as tall as mountains," said Sasha.

"And the streets are made of gold!" shouted Jacob.

Sasha and Anya held hands and swung around and around. Jacob gave a happy whoop.

We waved good-bye to the land until we couldn't see it any longer. Then we stared into the distance ahead. The Atlantic Ocean stretched as far as we could see. We were on our way to America.

CHAPTER 16
A Steerage Girl
Tatiana's Story

♥ ♥ ♥ ♥ ♥

The harbor had been calm. But once our ship entered the open sea, big waves began to roll. The mighty steamship groaned and creaked.

"Don't be scared," Anya whispered to me.

I *was* scared. But I was excited, too. I wanted to see America, where the streets were made of gold!

That first evening, there was music and dancing. Anya and Sasha pretended to waltz around the deck while I sat and watched.

The captain came to visit us. His dark uniform had rows of shiny buttons. At first, he reminded us of one of our enemies, the Cossack soldiers. However, the captain soon put us at ease.

He reached behind Anya's ear and pulled out a piece of candy!

"Magic tricks," said Anya in delight.

The captain handed the candy to Anya. Then he gave her a wink and a bow.

Everyone was so happy that we were on our way at

last. The entire Levov family came outside on the deck to enjoy the evening. We feasted on fish, bread with butter, and fruits. There were even pastries and cookies for dessert.

The smells of stew and boiled potatoes drifted up from the deck below us. Even the steerage passengers had come out to eat their simple supper and celebrate.

"Look!" Sasha pointed. It was the little girl in the yellow scarf. She and some other children were running races. "She is no longer fat!"

The girl won the race. Anya clapped.

The girl looked up and waved to us. She called out, but we could not understand her.

"She's Romanian," said Jacob. "I know a few words of her language."

The girl pointed up at a table near us. There was a bowl of bananas on it.

"Want one?" asked Anya. "Here! Catch!" Anya tossed a banana down to the girl.

The girl caught it in her apron. She picked up the banana and studied it. Then she looked at Anya with a question in her eyes.

"To eat!" Anya shouted. She pretended to eat invisible food.

The girl got the idea. She smiled and raised the banana to her lips. Then she took a big bite. She chewed the banana, skin and all!

The girl made a face. *"Bleah!"* She spat it back out.

Jacob and Sasha started laughing. Anya waved her hands, horrified. "No! No! Peel it first," she shouted. The girl shrugged to show she didn't understand.

Anya got another banana and ran back to the railing. She peeled the banana, so the girl could see. Then Anya took a bite.

The girl copied her, slowly peeling the banana. She took a little test bite of it. Then she smiled and gobbled the whole thing.

Mr. and Mrs. Levov came to see what was going on.

Mrs. Levov's face turned sour when she saw the girl on the deck below. She tugged Sasha away from the railing. "Hmmpf! A steerage girl. Dirty little thing. I suppose she can't help it, though. Steerage passengers don't have their own washrooms like we do."

"They are lucky if they even have a bed to themselves," said Mr. Levov. "It's tight quarters down there."

"Stay away from her, girls," warned Mrs. Levov. "Steerage is full of lice. And if you have lice, they might not let you into America."

"They keep you out for lice?" asked Anya.

Mrs. Levov nodded. "And for a great many other things as well. Some lice carry a disease called typhus. Only healthy people are allowed into America."

"On Ellis Island, doctors give everyone an eye test. They turn your eyelids inside out with a buttonhook!"

said Jacob. "I heard that they accidentally popped one man's eyeball out."

Anya and Sasha gasped.

"Jacob!" scolded Mrs. Levov.

"Don't worry," she told them. "The eye test is only for steerage. First class doesn't have to go to Ellis Island."

Anya looked down at the girl in the yellow scarf. I could tell what she was thinking. That poor girl would have to get the buttonhook eye test!

"Katia!" a woman shouted. The girl waved good-bye to Anya. Then she skipped toward the woman. Her mother, I supposed.

By the next morning, the rolling of the ship had made many people ill. All of the Levovs had become seasick. They could not even eat breakfast.

Anya and I were not ill, but we became bored. Sasha and Kira were sick in bed, so we had no one to play with.

Anya walked around our deck, watching the steerage families on the deck below. She was curious about them. I feared them a bit. There were so many! They spoke dozens of different languages. And some did not look clean.

By a stroke of good fortune, Katia was also among the few on our ship who were not seasick.

She saw us and ran over to stand just below us. She pointed at something in her hand. Then she tossed the thing up and over the railing toward us. Anya caught it.

It was a gift — a lovely shell! Inside, it was the same soft pink color as my cheeks.

In return, Anya tossed down another treat — an orange. This time, she showed Katia how to peel it first.

Next, Anya gave Katia a handful of unshelled nuts. Katia didn't eat them right away. Instead, she began tossing them in a circle. She was juggling!

Anya tried to copy her, but it was no use. Katia showed her how, over and over, until she got it. Anya laughed with delight.

Since Katia was Romanian, we could not understand her words. And she could not understand Anya's. But over the following days, Anya and Katia developed a code. They pointed and talked with hand signals. Anya gave Katia treats of food when she could, and Katia often gave her small gifts in return.

Their friendship grew, though they stayed on their separate decks. Katia helped Anya feel less lonely.

One day as we were nearing the end of our voyage, the sea began rolling badly. Many were still seasick. But not Anya, Katia, or I. When Anya spotted Katia down on the steerage deck, she skipped toward the railing.

The ship gave a sudden lurch, and Anya tripped. She could not hold on to me! I was knocked from her arms.

I dropped over the railing and fell down, down, down to the deck below.

CHAPTER 17

Lady Liberty

Tatiana's Story

♥ ♥ ♥ ♥ ♥

Whack!

My face! My beautiful face! I felt it crack.

But I had little time to worry about that. There was danger all around me. Sturdy boots clomped by, nearly crushing me. Footwear of every kind went past. I saw shiny leather shoes with buckles and heels. Cracked shoes full of holes. Ragged cloth shoes held together with twine. Even wooden clogs.

"Lady Liberty!" someone shouted. People rushed to one side of the ship. They wanted to see the famous Statue of Liberty.

The deck rattled from the pounding of running feet. I bounced with every step. No one looked down to see me lying there.

My face ached. I moaned. Where was Anya?

Soon a pair of gentle hands scooped me up. I was saved!

But it wasn't Anya who held me. It was Katia. Her worried eyes searched for Anya on the first-class deck above. Anya wasn't at the railing any longer.

Katia frowned. She whispered to me. I couldn't understand her language. Her voice was kind, but I was still afraid.

Suddenly Anya was there beside us. She cradled me in her arms and touched my cheek. "Oh, poor Tatiana. I am so sorry. Don't worry. It is only a small crack. You are still beautiful."

I hoped it was true. I wanted to get back to our cabin and see for myself in the mirror.

Then I realized something horrible. We were on the steerage deck! The Levovs had warned Anya not to come here. Would we get lice? Would it stop us from getting into America?

The crush of people continued. We were swept along, moving away from the stairs that led up to the first-class deck.

"Lady Liberty!" voices cried out. Some were laughing. Others were crying with joy. I tried to see what everyone was looking at, but there were people on all sides. I couldn't see the sky unless I looked straight up.

Anya and Katia climbed up onto a coil of thick rope, for a better view.

An amazing sight greeted us then. A grand green

lady holding a torch stood in the ocean on the left side of our ship. She seemed to rise out of the sea to stand as tall as a building.

"It's the Statue of Liberty," whispered Anya. "It means we are here. We're in America, Tatiana!"

Just past the statue, our ship docked at the tip of New York City's Manhattan Island. On the deck above us, the first-class and second-class passengers began leaving the ship. But no one in steerage was allowed to get off.

An angry voice in the crowd shouted, "Why can't we go now, too?"

"Only first- and second-class passengers are allowed off here," said a crewman. "You'll get off on Ellis Island. That is our next stop."

I looked in the direction he was pointing. I saw a red brick and white stone building with four copper-domed towers. That fancy palace was Ellis Island?

Anya pointed up at the first-class deck. "I have to go back up," she told Katia.

Katia helped Anya push her way to the bottom of the stairs.

At last! Anya hugged Katia good-bye. Then she ran up the stairs. We had to catch up with the Levovs before the ship sailed for Ellis Island.

"Mr. Levov!" Anya called. "Sasha! Kira!"

Halfway up the stairs, a crewman blocked our way.

"Let me pass! I belong up here. I'm sailing in first class," said Anya.

The sailor smiled and shook his head. He raised both hands, palms up. He didn't understand us. He spoke some words in English. We didn't understand him.

He would not let us by.

Anya tried to duck under his arm. We almost got around him. But he caught us. The crewman was not smiling now. He turned Anya around and marched her down the stairs.

"You don't understand —" began Anya.

He gave Anya a rude little push.

And then we were trapped on the steerage deck once again. It was a nightmare.

The first- and second-class decks were soon empty. The Levovs had left without us. In the crowd, they must not have noticed we were missing!

"My things! The letter from Father was in my bag," Anya cried. "How will we ever find my uncle Elias in America now?"

Our ship set sail for Ellis Island, across the bay. Everyone grew silent. We were all wondering the same thing. Would America let us in?

Anya and I stood on the deck in a crowd of a thousand people. But we were alone.

CHAPTER 18

Ellis Island

Tatiana's Story

♥ ♥ ♥ ♥ ♥

A small hand reached out and grabbed Anya's. Katia!

Katia pulled Anya along through the crowd and down the stairs into steerage. Mrs. Levov had been right. Steerage was a disgusting place. There were rows and rows of narrow beds, stacked three high. There were no windows. And it smelled like fish stew and vomit!

Katia didn't seem to notice. She pulled us along the rows to one of the beds. She shook a girl sleeping there and spoke to her. The girl sat up and began coughing. She looked ill. I thought this must be Katia's sister.

Katia unwrapped a bundle of clothes. Then one by one, she pulled dresses over her head. One, two, three. Katia was fat again.

Anya laughed. "Now I understand. Wearing four dresses is easier than carrying them!"

Katia grinned and nodded. Then she pulled us back up the stairs with her. Katia's sister followed. Up on deck, Katia's mother seemed surprised to see Anya and me. She looked from Anya to the empty first-class deck above us and frowned.

She tucked Katia and us close to her. We held onto Katia's mother's skirts as we all got off the ship. None of us wanted to get lost in the crowds.

Our ship was too large to dock at Ellis Island. So we were loaded onto flat-bottomed ferryboats that took us there.

The first room we entered at Ellis Island was filled with baggage, from floor to ceiling. Here many left their trunks, baskets, and bundles to be picked up later. It was a sad reminder of Anya's bag, which we had lost on the steamship.

Next we climbed a grand stairway. Doctors at the top studied us as we walked. They wrote a P with blue chalk on Katia's sister's dark coat.

They wrote letters on other people as well. I saw a B, an E, and an H. I had learned some English letters from Anya. She had studied the English alphabet in school.

"What does it mean?" asked Anya.

No one answered.

The doctors had pulled Katia's sister out of the line. Katia's mother insisted on going with her, so Katia went, too. Katia, her mother, and her sister went one way.

Anya was pulled another. We were alone in the crowd. Again.

2326

Anya and I and hundreds of others were herded like cattle into a room with a ceiling two stories high. Sunlight poured in through huge round-topped windows. Metal railings and wire fences divided the room's tiled floor into a maze of rows. We were told to line up and wait.

Around and around the rows we went, weaving back and forth. We heard strange languages all around us. It was so noisy Anya tucked me under her arm and put her hands over her ears. We waited and waited.

There was a lot of time to think and worry. What if we could not get into America? What if we were sent back to Russia? What if we could not find Anya's uncle? What if her father and Baba never came? What if? What if?

Move and sit. Sit and move. I grew tired of it. Where were we going?

Then I saw.

Up ahead stood a man with a buttonhook.

Anya saw him at the same time I did. "No!" She began to cry.

Stop crying! I whispered. *It will make your eyes red, and the doctors might think you are sick. Then they won't let us stay in America.*

Another man in a dark uniform came toward us. He frowned and looked around us for Anya's parents. He saw no one, of course, because we had no one.

"Where are your father and mother?" the man asked. He spoke Russian!

But Anya was too scared to answer.

After a moment, the man turned and spoke to me instead. "And who is this?" he asked.

How lucky I was to meet one of those rare humans who could speak to my kind. Joyfully, I answered. *We are Tatiana and Anya Peskin. We are lost. Please, can you —*

The man ignored my outburst. He turned back to Anya. "What's your dolly's name?" he asked her.

How rude! The man had only pretended to speak to me. He had never expected me to answer at all.

"Are you from Russia?" he asked Anya.

Somehow Anya found the courage to speak. Once she began, she couldn't stop. "I am Anya Peskin from Russia. My father sent me to America with Mr. Levov. We traveled on the ship in first class. Then Mr. Levov got off, and I got trapped on the steerage deck. I am going to live with my uncle Elias in New York. He would come and get me. But he doesn't know I'm here on Ellis Island."

"Don't worry," said the man. "We will find your uncle." He stamped a piece of paper and pinned it on Anya's coat. It said: Detained.

What did that mean?

Someone took us to a smaller waiting room that was

full of women and children. Beds were stacked on the sides of the room, ready to be pulled out at night. At one end of the room, a guard stood watch.

"Anya!" someone cried.

Anya turned. "Katia! How did you get here?"

Katia explained with hand signals, as best she could.

It seemed that Katia's sister was sick. That's what the chalk letters had meant! A different letter for each illness.

Katia and her mother had to wait until Katia's sister got well before they could all leave Ellis Island. I was sorry Katia's sister was sick. But selfishly, I was glad Katia was with us again.

CHAPTER 19
Independence Day
Tatiana's Story

♥ ♥ ♥ ♥ ♥

That evening, the guards pulled the beds out into the middle of the room. Katia and Anya chose beds next to each other, and we all lay down, exhausted. It was odd, but I still felt the rocking of the ship even though we were now on land.

Later that night, Katia's moans woke us. Anya felt her friend's forehead.

"You are burning hot! I'll get your mother," said Anya. She used her hands to show Katia what she meant.

"No!" Katia grabbed Anya and looked at her with pleading eyes. I knew why she didn't want to tell. If anyone found out she was sick, it would take even longer until her family could leave Ellis Island. Or even worse, she might have to go back to Romania if she never got well.

But Anya and I were worried. What if Katia were really, really ill? She might need some medicine. If she didn't get it, she might get even more sick.

Pop! Pop! Pop! Loud cracking sounds split the night.

What now? My first thought was of the Cossacks and their guns! Had the cruel soldiers followed us to America?

Anya hopped onto her bed to look out the high window.

Get down! I cried. *Get away from the window. You might be killed by the soldiers' bullets.*

"Oh! It's beautiful!" Anya whispered. She helped Katia up to look. Other children gathered around to look as well.

"What is it?" breathed a Russian girl.

Yes! What is it? What is it? I willed Anya to hear me. I wanted to see, too. Finally she remembered me. She lifted me high enough to look out the window.

Outside, the night sky crackled and sparkled with hundreds of lights. Red, white, and blue star bursts exploded in the sky. Pinwheels of light sizzled and then burned away.

The leftover smoke drifted toward us in the breeze. I could not help shaking. I remembered the smoke from other fires back home in Russia.

"They're fireworks!" explained the guard in English. "It's the Fourth of July, America's Independence Day."

We didn't understand her words. It was impossible to ask questions. So we just enjoyed the show.

Far into the night we could see sparklers and hear

fireworks pop. The lights of buildings on the shore of New York City danced across the water.

We stayed awake as long as we could.

Early the next morning, we were wakened by a new guard who spoke Russian. She was smiling with good news.

"Anya Peskin?" she called. "Your uncle Elias was contacted by officials and is here to get you. He brings word that your father and grandmother are on their way to America. You have a few minutes to get dressed. I will come back for you and take you to your uncle."

Happiness filled me. We would soon be rescued!

Anya hopped out of bed and dressed in a hurry. Then she leaned over to Katia. In my excitement, I had forgotten her.

Katia was awake and watching us.

Anya pointed at herself to show she meant "I." She pointed toward one of thc guards and the door beyond. "I am leaving and must say good-bye," she said.

Katia understood. Tears slid down her cheeks. I knew she was happy for us. But she was worried for herself. And it was sad to say good-bye.

Anya touched Katia's forehead. Her face was still pink and hot.

Anya frowned with worry. Would she tell someone about Katia's illness? I held my breath, wondering.

Katia's eyes were wide. *Don't tell*, they seemed to beg.

Anya stayed silent and simply held Katia's hand. Katia dozed off as we waited for the guard.

"Hurry, Anya," the guard called moments later. "It is time to go."

Anya stared down at Katia and then back at me. After a brief struggle within herself, I could tell she had reached a decision.

She hugged me tighter than she ever had before. She kissed my cracked cheek. "I will miss you, my forever friend," she said.

At first I thought she was speaking to Katia. Then I realized she was speaking to me!

Suddenly I guessed what she was about to do. I was sad. But I was also proud of her for her kindness.

Anya tucked me under the bedcovers beside Katia as she lay sleeping.

"Take good care of Katia," Anya whispered to me. "Stay with her always."

I will, I whispered.

I watched my girl walk away with the guard, toward America. Anya was on her way to an exciting new land. A new life. Without me.

I stayed behind with Katia. She was a sweet girl, and she had been good to my Anya. I would give her what comfort I could.

It was the last time I ever saw my girl, Anya.

But I never forgot her.

CHAPTER 20
New Again

♥ ♥ ♥ ♥ ♥

"All done," Far Nana said in a satisfied voice. She had just airbrushed pink blush onto Tatiana's cheeks. It dried right away.

Rose and Lila blinked, trying to get used to being in the present time again.

Far Nana took off the cloth she had wrapped around Tatiana's body to protect her new clothes from the paint. She placed Tatiana on the windowsill and stepped back to admire her. Rose and Lila came closer to see.

"It's a miracle," said Rose.

Tatiana's pink cheek was smooth and no longer cracked. Her velvet skirt and lacy blouse had been mended. Stiff petticoats made a swishing sound under her skirt.

"She's new again!" said Lila.

"But Tatiana's story was sooo sad!" said Rose.

"Why didn't you make it have a happy ending?" asked Lila.

"It is what it is," said Far Nana. "I can't change history."

Rose and Lila still didn't quite believe Far Nana could hear Tatiana. They thought she might be making it all up. Neither of them was sure how to ask her. It would be like calling Far Nana a liar!

Rinnng!

Far Nana picked up the phone. "Hello? Hello, Nadia." She listened for a while. "Yes. Tatiana is well. She's ready to go home. All right. See you soon."

Far Nana hung up.

Rose and Lila stared at her.

"You mean Tatiana is leaving?" asked Rose.

"Of course," said Far Nana. She pulled a piece of paper from a stack on her desk. It said *Certificate of Wellness* in fancy gold lettering. She filled in the date and Tatiana's name. Then she rolled up the paper and tied a ribbon around it.

"All the dolls go home to their families once I make them well," Far Nana continued. "Just like patients in a people hospital do."

"Why isn't Tatiana going back home to Anya?" asked Lila.

"Anya gave her to Katia, remember?" said Far Nana.

"Then why isn't she going back to Katia?" asked Rose. "Who's Nadia?"

Lila gasped. "Oh, no! I just thought of something awful. Did Katia die at Ellis Island?"

"No, Katia lived a long and happy life," said Far

Nana. "She and her sister got well and entered America one week after Anya. But that was all a hundred years ago."

Rose spread her arms wide. "So how did Tatiana get here? This is a long way from Ellis Island."

"Katia gave Tatiana to her daughter. And her daughter gave Tatiana to her daughter. Tatiana was passed through the family over the years. And now she lives with Katia's great-great-granddaughter, Nadia," said Far Nana.

Just then, someone knocked on the front door.

"That's probably her now," said Far Nana. She picked up Tatiana and the certificate and headed for the door.

Rose and Lila tiptoed from the witch's hat and sat on the stairs. They peeked down, trying to see Tatiana's owner without being seen. Ringo crawled into Lila's lap.

Lila poked Rose. "Can you see anything? What are they saying?"

Rose grabbed Lila's finger to stop the poking. "Shhh! I'm trying to listen."

"I wish Tatiana didn't have to go," grumbled Lila. "Everybody's always leaving us."

Lila was right. Everybody did seem to be leaving them lately. It made Rose feel jittery inside. But she didn't let Lila know.

"Mom, Dad, and now Tatiana," Lila continued. "Far

Nana will probably move away, too. Maybe she'll move in with Tatiana and Nadia. Then we'll be all alone in this creepy house."

"Don't forget John, Paul, George, and Ringo," said Rose.

"Big whoop," said Lila. She petted Ringo so he wouldn't take it personally.

"Mom and Dad will come back," Rose told Lila. "They promised. And look on the bright side. Instead of three hundred sixty-five days until we see them, now it's just three hundred sixty-three!"

"Girls, come meet Nadia!" Far Nana called.

Rose and Lila jumped.

"Should we pretend not to hear?" asked Lila. "I don't want to say another good-bye — to Tatiana, I mean."

"No. Let's go down," Rose said. "I want to see who gets to keep Tatiana."

A girl with long dark brown braids stood talking to Far Nana at the front door.

Lila elbowed Rose as they went down the stairs.

"Yeah, I know," whispered Rose. "It's that spy girl from next door."

"What are you doing here?" Nadia said when she saw them.

"We live here now — for a while," said Rose.

Lila moved closer to Far Nana. She tried to get between her and Nadia.

"I live in the yellow house next door," said Nadia.

Lila squinted at her. "We know."

"So, isn't that great," Far Nana said in a fakey, extra-cheerful way. Rose had figured out that was her nervous voice. "Maybe Nadia will invite you girls over to visit Tatiana one day."

Rinnng!

"Two phone calls in ten minutes," said Far Nana. "A record. It's usually so quiet around here. Things have been hopping since you girls came."

Far Nana sounded like she wasn't sure "hopping" was a good way for things to be. *Too bad,* thought Rose. She was stuck with them. Just like they were stuck with her. And Rose wasn't sure she liked it, either.

Far Nana's voice faded away as she went into the living room to answer the phone.

Nobody knew what to say once Far Nana left.

Then Nadia mumbled, "I guess you could come over sometime. If you want. I mean, summer is kind of boring. All there is to do is watch TV."

"TV!?" echoed Rose and Lila.

Joy, oh, joy, thought Rose. "Okay, maybe," she said.

Lila played it cool, too. "We'll try to come over when we're not busy helping in the doll hospital."

"Your grandmother lets you help?" said Nadia. "Wow. She made my doll look *sooo* good. I bet Tatiana looked just like this when she sailed to America with my great-great grandmother."

Rose and Lila stared in surprise. Could Far Nana's Tatiana story be true?

"Well, see you. I want to show Tatiana to my mom." Nadia went down the porch steps, with Tatiana in her arms.

"Wait! What was your great-great grandmother's name?" Rose called after her.

Rose and Lila gasped as Nadia's answer floated back to them.

"Katia," she said.

CHAPTER 21
Looking Up

♥ ♥ ♥ ♥ ♥

It's your mom and dad," said Far Nana, coming back into the front hall.

It took Rose a second to shift gears. But not Lila.

"Yippee!" shouted Lila. "They called like they promised."

She ran past Far Nana. Rose followed close behind. The race was on.

Lila came to a dead stop just inside the living room. Rose bumped into her, and they skidded across the waxed wood floor.

"Where is it?" shouted Lila. "The phone — where is it?"

"Behind the spider plants in the hanging macramé holders," Far Nana shouted back.

Rose spotted it first. But Lila was faster. She grabbed the phone and answered.

Rose gave Lila The Eye.

Lila grinned back. "Hello? Mom! Dad!"

She let Rose listen to half the phone.

"It's the middle of the night here," said their mom. "We stayed up late to call you girls. How are things going?"

"We get to stay in your room, Mom. And Far Nana has cats!" said Lila.

Their dad laughed.

"Sounds like things are going well," said their mom.

"So far," added Rose.

They heard some scratchy sounds on the phone.

"We're on a speakerphone, and we're losing our connection," said their mom. "So we're going to say bye for now, but we'll call you again soon. Be good for your grandmother. We love you."

"Okay, bye," said Lila. "Love you, too."

Rose grabbed the phone all to herself. "Mom? Dad? Are you still there?"

"Yes," they both answered.

"Don't ask why," she said. "Just listen and do something, okay? Ready?"

"I guess so. Ready," said her mom and dad.

"Okay, wrap your left arm around under your right arm. And your right arm under your left," Rose told them.

"Did you do it?" asked Rose.

"Yes," they said.

"That's a hug," said Rose. "From me. I forgot to give it to you before you left."

Her parents laughed.

There were more scratchy sounds, and then the phone conked out.

Lila whirled around and around in the orange bowl chair, singing. "Over the ocean, inside a plane, to Africa Mom and Dad go . . ."

Rose gave her another push. Then she sang, ". . . Far Nana knows the way to make sick dolls okay . . ."

Then Lila again: ". . . But do dolls really tell her what they know, ho?"

Boing! Boing! Boing!

Lila stopped whirling. "What was that?"

They went to see.

One of the gray cats was knocking a doll eyeball down the stairs. *Boing! Boing! Boing!*

It landed by Rose's and Lila's feet, staring up.

Far Nana joined them, and they all looked at it.

"One of your doll eyeballs is *stairing*," Rose joked.

Far Nana laughed. "So *eye* see."

"Things are starting to *look up* around here," added Lila.

They all giggled.

Things certainly were.

Glossary

bisque porcelain that is not very shiny

buttonhook a small, simple tool with a hook on one end, used to pull buttons through buttonholes

ceramic materials such as clay that are used to make dolls and pottery

china shiny porcelain

Ellis Island an immigration station on a small island in New York Harbor, near the southern tip of Manhattan and the Statue of Liberty. Buildings on Ellis Island included a huge main registration hall, a hospital, a laundry, and a kitchen.

first class rooms on a ship that are the biggest, best, and most expensive

immigrants people who leave one country and go to live in another country

kiln a special oven used for baking ceramic and porcelain at very hot temperatures

pogroms organized attacks on Jews in Russia in the early 1900s

porcelain a fine-grained ceramic material that is heated in a kiln and is breakable

second class rooms on a ship that are not as big or expensive as those in first class but that are better than the space in steerage

Statue of Liberty a large green-colored statue of a woman holding a torch high in one hand. She stands in New York Harbor.

steerage lowest, crowded, basementlike part of a ship in which passengers traveled for the least amount of money

Questions and Answers About Immigrants and Ellis Island

Why did immigrants come to the United States of America?

People in many countries were poor. They moved to the United States hoping to find jobs, earn money, and make better lives for themselves.

In some countries, people were punished for their religion. They hoped to practice their religion without fear in the United States.

How many immigrants came to America?

Twenty million immigrants came to the United States between 1892 and 1924. Many came from Germany, England, Ireland, France, Italy, and Sweden. More than three million came from Russia. That was the most from any country!

Anya and Tatiana sailed to America in 1907, the busiest year of immigration. More than a million people came to the United States that year.

What did immigrants bring to America?
They brought toys, clothes, dishes, religious items, blankets, family pictures, and more. What would you bring if you were moving and could only take as much as you could carry?

What happened to immigrants on Ellis Island?
Most immigrants spent an average of five hours on Ellis Island, but an immigrant could be kept there for days or weeks. Immigrants were detained for illness or for other problems. Immigrants who were too sick to enter the United States had to return by ship to their own country. If an immigrant child had to return home, a parent usually had to go with the child.

Ellis Island was nicknamed the Island of Tears. That's because many immigrants were afraid. Moving to a new country was scary. They didn't know what to expect. They worried that America might not welcome them. And they worried that they might be sent back home.

The United States only wanted healthy immigrants who could earn a living by working. Doctors marked a letter on the clothes of people who seemed to have an illness or other problem. Then other doctors examined those immigrants more closely to see if they really were sick. Some of the letters of the code were: B for back; E,

Eyes; H, heart; P, physical or lung problems; X, mental illness.

Immigrants were given an eye test to find out if they had an eye disease called trachoma. A doctor lifted their eyelids with a buttonhook to check for redness.

Most officials were helpful and kind to the immigrants. Interpreters spoke eighteen languages. There was plenty of food. Immigrants on Ellis Island were given meals of bread and butter, eggs, milk, beef stew, potatoes, corned beef hash, and fruit. Many of them had never seen bananas or oranges, so they weren't sure how to eat them.

Were immigrants happy in America?

Most immigrants wanted to fit in to their new country. They tried to dress and speak like Americans. Children went to school to learn English.

Immigrants got jobs and worked hard in the United States. Even children worked to earn money for their families. They sold flowers and newspapers on the streets. They delivered telegrams on bicycles. They worked in factories.

Some immigrants returned home to their former countries, but most were happy to stay in America.

Watch for the next book in the

Doll Hospital™ series,

Saving Marissa

coming soon.

Rose hid her face in her hands. "If anybody finds out I spent today at day care, I'll die."

Her grandmother's long paisley skirt swirled as she opened the door to the van. "I'm sorry, but it's the best I could do at the last minute. I forgot there's no school today. And I have to go to a meeting."

Rose's little sister, Lila, stared at the house where they'd parked. "Is this the day care? It just looks like a normal house. Except for the sign out front that says Doodle Dandy Day Care." She sounded disappointed.

"What did you expect?" asked their grandmother.

Lila shrugged. "More baby stuff, I guess." She grabbed her dog-shaped backpack, jumped out of the van, and headed for the front porch.

Rose checked inside her backpack for her book and the other things she needed. Her fingers touched something soft and fuzzy. Her secret.

The charms on Rose's backpack clinked together as they all walked along the sidewalk. Rose tried one last time to change her grandmother's mind. "We don't need a baby-sitter. I can take care of Lila and me for one measly day."

Her grandmother didn't answer.

Rose went up the steps to the porch, not quite stomping. But almost. "I'm ten, remember? I'm too old for a baby-sitter," she said.

"You're too young to stay home on your own," said her grandmother.

"Besides, this isn't a baby-sitter. It's day care," said Lila.

Rose rolled her eyes. "Don't remind me."

Lila rang the doorbell. The chimes played "Rock-a-bye Baby." Lila hummed along.

Rose groaned.

Inside the house, footsteps thundered closer.

"Goodness," said their grandmother. "Sounds like a herd of buffalo in there."

"Buffalo babies, probably," said Rose.

The door opened and a smiling woman with short gray hair greeted them. She wore pants with numbers on them and a shirt covered with the ABCs.

A little girl with red hair peeked around the woman on one side. She held up three fingers. "I'm fwee!" she told them.

A little boy squeezed past on the woman's other side. He stopped sucking his thumb and pointed at Rose and Lila. "Big kids," he said.

"I phoned a few minutes ago about bringing Rose and Lila over for the day," their grandmother explained.

"Oh, yes! Come on in," said the woman. She gently herded the little boy and girl away from the door.

Rose and Lila's grandmother nudged them into the house.

Photo by George Hallowell

JOAN HOLUB

About the Author

When Joan Holub was a girl, her best friend, Ann, lived right down the street. Ann had lots of toys. But she had one special doll that Joan loved best — a beautiful ballerina. It had lace-up shoes and a frilly satin tutu. Its body was jointed and bendable.

After a few years, Joan's family moved away. Ann gave the doll to Joan as a going-away present. Joan named the doll Annie, after her friend.

Joan played with Annie so much that she eventually wore her out. Annie's arms and legs came apart. She needed help! So Joan and her mother took Annie to a doll hospital. There, Annie's arms and legs were put back together. She even got a new wig.

Annie and some of her doll friends live in Washington State with Joan, her husband, George, and their two cats.

Joan Holub is the author and/or illustrator of many books for children. You can find out more about Joan and her books on her Web site, *www.joanholub.com.*